Stop, Fox!

Time to Read™ is an early reader program designed to guide children to literacy success regardless of age or grade level. The program's three levels correspond to stages of reading readiness, making book selection straightforward, and assuring that when it's time for a child to read, the right book is waiting.

| — Level — 1 | **Beginning to Read** | • Large, simple type | • Word repetition |
| | | • Basic vocabulary | • Strong illustration support |

| — Level — 2 | **Reading with Help** | • Short sentences | • Simple dialogue |
| | | • Engaging stories | • Illustration support |

| — Level — 3 | **Reading Independently** | • Longer sentences | • Short paragraphs |
| | | • Harder words | • Increased story complexity |

For Antonio, super sloth fan!
—LHH

For Dara and Walter—AW

Library of Congress Cataloging-in-Publication data
is on file with the publisher.

Text copyright © 2019 by Lori Haskins Houran
Illustrations copyright © 2019 by Albert Whitman & Company
Illustrated by Alex Willmore
First published in the United States of America
in 2019 by Albert Whitman & Company
ISBN 978-0-8075-7209-2

Printed in China
10 9 8 7 6 5 4 3 2 1 HH 24 23 22 21 20 19

Design by Morgan Beck

For more information about Albert Whitman & Company,
visit our website at www.albertwhitman.com.

100 Years of Albert Whitman & Company
Celebrate with us in 2019!

Stop, Fox!

Lori Haskins Houran

illustrated by
Alex Willmore

Albert Whitman & Company
Chicago, Illinois

Fox talks.
A LOT.

“Stop, Fox!”
says Ape.

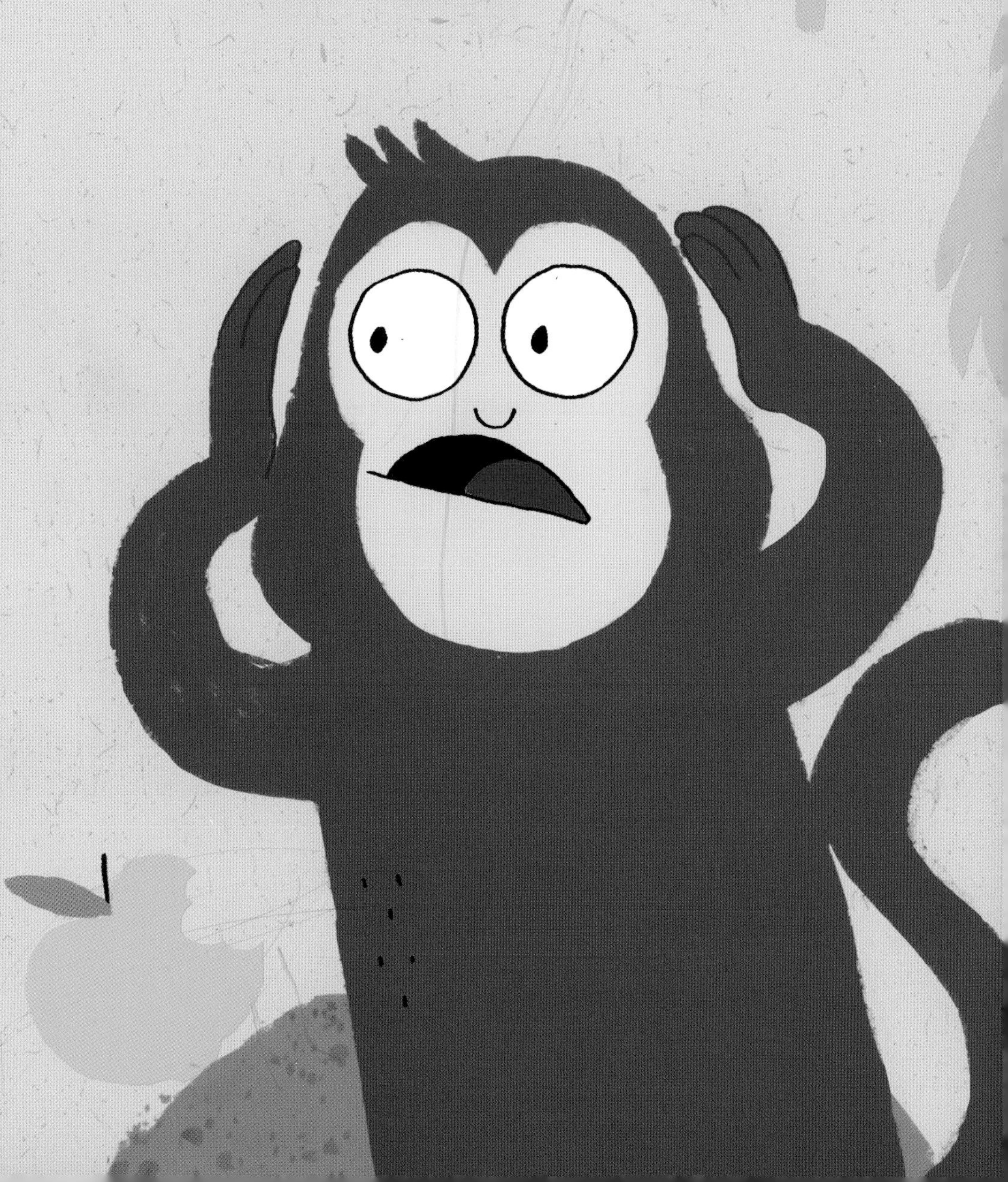

"Stop, Fox!"
says Bird.

"Stop, Fox!"
says Cub.

Fox stops.
Fox walks.

Fox sees Sloth.
Fox talks.

Sloth does NOT
say stop!

"Talk, Fox!"
says Sloth.
"It helps me sleep."

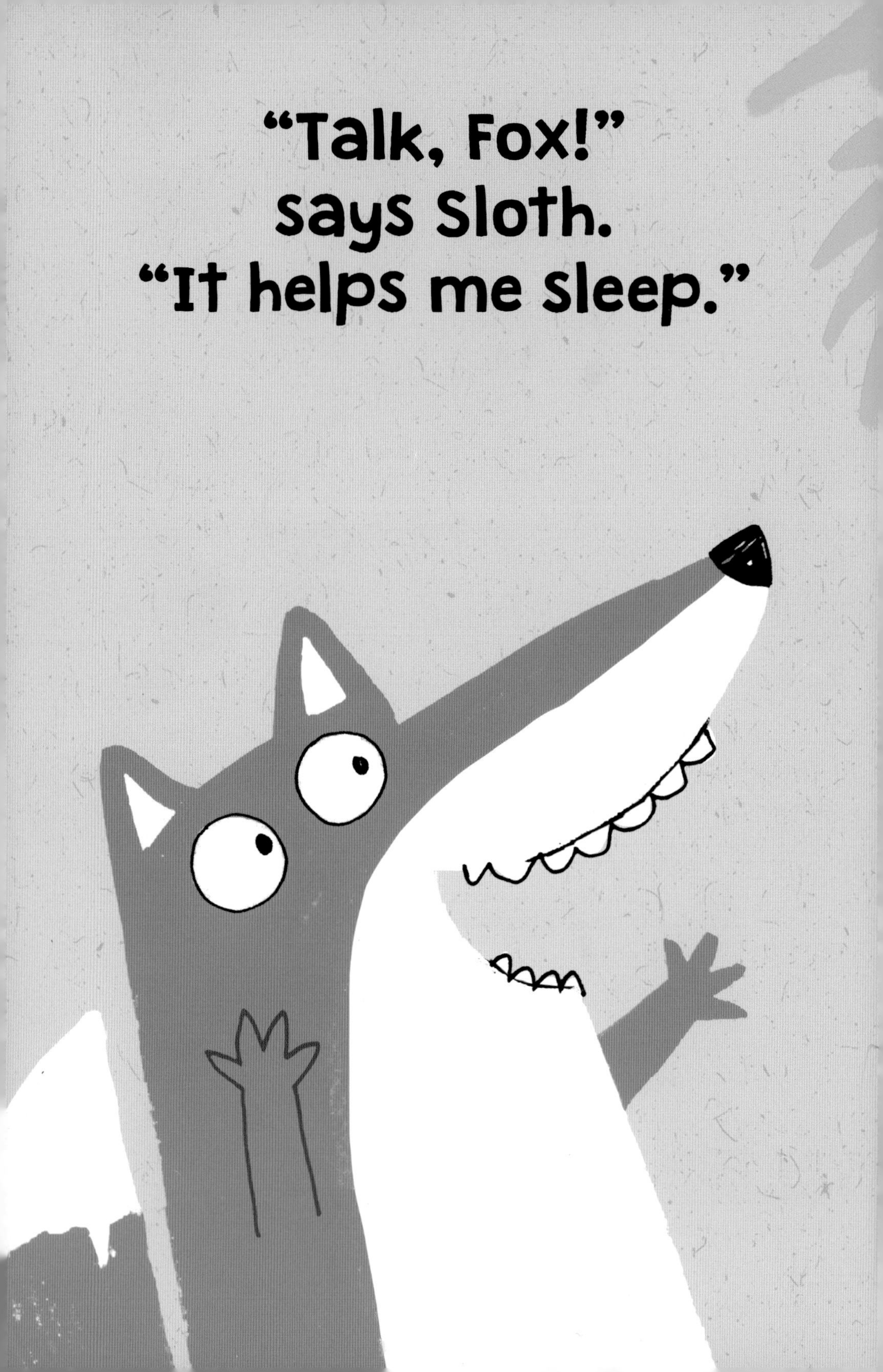

Fox talks.
And talks.

And talks.
And talks.
And talks.

Sloth sleeps.
Fox stops.

"Talk, Fox!"
says Sloth.

Fox talks.
And talks.

And talks.
And talks.
And—

walks.

"Fox?"
says Sloth.

Fox RUNS!

Ape feels bad.
Bird feels bad.
Cub feels bad.

They did not let
Fox talk.

Fox runs by.

"Talk, Fox?"
says Cub.

Fox does not stop.

"Talk, Fox?"
says Bird.

Fox does not stop.

"Talk, Fox?"
says Ape.

Fox does not stop.

At last, Fox stops.

Fox sleeps.
A LOT.

And Sloth?

Sloth smiles.